Inspired by The Queen's Gambit

1. Mental Collapse

Emily Walsh is sat alone in her front room of her Brooklyn apartment. It's night time. The curtains are closed. The lights are off. It's dark and so is her mind. She has been triggered and her mind has habitually shut down. This is a regular occurrence for Emily. The energy has been drained from her fragile psyche. If you looked into her mind right now you would find no passion for anything. You would find depression, irritability, and no zest for life. But Emily isn't psychotic. She isn't always useless like this. She isn't always broken like this. So even when she is like this there is very high probability of recovery. The prognosis is always excellent. She is aware that eventually she will muster the fight to once again, recover. But for now it feels impossible. She will inevitably experience uncomfortable dreams tonight.

Emily's fragile ego insists on predictability. She possesses an habitual mindset that is addicted to various positions on things. She cannot be contradicted otherwise she experiences the dissociation or collapse of her mind. There are plenty of thoughts in Emily's mind that must not be contradicted. Indeed, there are too many position that must not be contradicted. So just like it is inevitable that she will recover, it is equally inevitable that she will again collapse. Collapse occurs with as much certainty as night follows day.

So why did that guy at the snooker club have to go and say that she is screwed up? Emily's defense mechanism kicked in at that point and caused a change in her mind from agreeability with life to feeling like life had come to an end. The irony here is that her over-reaction proves his point. But Emily is not one to challenge herself. She is not one to reflect on her neurosis. She doesn't do talking therapy. She doesn't do analysis. She is addicted to her minds attitude thus she defends it. Any contradicting of her thoughts is taken as an attack. And yet, on one thing… she is more than willing to challenge herself, reflect on herself, adapt her thoughts and beliefs, and analyse her views. That one thing being snooker. When she restores her ego her energy will return, agreeability with life will return and her analytical ability will return and her passion will return. All will come back online. But all of that energy, agreeability, analytical ability and passion will be like a planet revolving around one thing and one thing alone… its Sun… and in this case the Sun = Snooker. The problem with the planet moving again is that it will not last. She'll be triggered and collapse again. And that is Emily Walsh' stop-start bi-polar life.

2. Snooker Genius

Emily doesn't acknowledge that she's neurotic. But for the rest of us, we would say that rightly or wrongly, as a child, she didn't feel like others were supportive of her. Thus she did not trust. There is no big and obvious trigger such as parents dying in a car crash and thus feelings of abandonment. Her feelings of abandonment derive from a more dubious perspective of her's. One might say from a paranoid perspective. But nevertheless, they are just as real to her. Failure to challenge her ego's positions are both self-defeating and yet simultaneously, to be credited where Emily's genius snooker abilities are concerned. As its her obsession to snooker that could make her famous, successful and very rich. This passion for snooker is due to finding the snooker halls as a hiding-place for her both as a child and now as an 18 year old young adult. And she just loves the game as she is a unique natural talent. And she knows it. The existence of snooker halls were discovered by the young Emily when on vacation as a child in England. Her dad would play a-little, due to his curiosity about how difficult it is compared to pool. He discovered the answer to be that is is much more difficult than pool. Emily joined in playing snooker, and naturally despite being tall for her age, required a little stool to be able to reach at times. But for some unbeknown reason she was able to play well from the very start. She would demand of her parents that she play there for as long as possible while in England and the luck of being from Brooklyn, New York meant that she could find somewhere in the City that had snooker tables. And as a child she would spend all her spare time there funded by her parents. At age 9 she amazed a 40 year old man and trusted family friend called Michael Saunders. when she made a century break. "Impossible" he said as she potted the ball that meant she had made a break of 100. He then said "Emily, you are not normal at this game". Emily responded "How good am I?" Michael looks her and thinks to himself, incredible, she's only 9 years old. He walks over to Emily and crouches down to her level. He stares right into her eyes and says "To tell you the truth Emily, you're astounding." Michael did not need to coach Emily. She was a natural. He was there when she made her first 147 aged 14. He (and everyone else) in the building had come over as Emily's opponent had made

4

everyone aware that this young girl is on a potential 147. The entire hall erupted into the loudest cheer it had ever heard when she potted the final black.

Both her century and her 147 breaks were made at the Athletic Club in New York City. Conveniently for Emily this is where the National U.S. Snooker Championship is held. Her parents had insisted she wait until she has completed her education before she attempts a career at snooker. They had underestimated her talent, this despite her genius, because they did not understand the sport. This caused a serious rift between Emily and her parents and by July 2023 she had split from them aged 18 when she discovered a way to become independent using her talent as a snooker and pool genius. It was at that point that she moved into her Brooklyn apartment.

Emily made plenty of money. She took advantage of the fact that she could never get around every single NYC bar (with a pool table) if she tried. This meant that she had a never-ending menu to choose from concerning bars with pool tables. And although, not 21, she looked 21 and was therefore like many young women of that age, not suspected of being underage when entering bars. Besides, she was not there to drink alcohol. She is tee-total. She is simply there to kick ass and cash-out. And that is precisely what she did time and time again.

It's October 2023. For several months Emily has earned over $150 a day by betting guys that she meets that she will beat them at pool. She's just going from NYC bar to NYC bar. If they don't have a pool table she will just walk out and go elsewhere.

Emily enters O' Hanlon's Bar. She doesn't even bother to order a drink. She notices that a pool game is just ending and that the loser of the game has had enough and is leaving. The winner also seems to be leaving until Emily approaches him and asks for a game. The guy, Luke, finds Emily attractive. She is tall, a little on the slim side, with long blonde flowing hair making her appear, if you judge on looks, much more confident and stable than she really is. Luke accepts. Emily deliberately plays poor enough to ensure that Luke wins. On potting the final black he feigns a-little modesty by saying

"They don't call me Lucky Luke for nothing".

Emily smiles and says

"I bet 20 dollars I can beat you in the next game."

She slams 20 dollars on the side of the table. Luke slowly puts his drink down and asks

"Are you sure? I don't know if I am comfortable taking your money."

"But you were just *lucky Luke* remember."

Dollar signs light up in Luke's eyes, out-weighing his concern for taking Emily's money so he says

"Deal" and slams 20 dollars on the table.

Emily broke off and potted a stripe. Luke thinks he will have a chance to pot a solid very soon. But Emily simply clears the table, whitewashing unlucky Luke. She picks up $40 on the side of the table, and says bye. Before looking back at him and saying

"We can play again if you want?"

Luke shook his head. But another guy, who hadn't seen the game calls her back saying

"I'll play."

"How much for?" asks Emily.

The guy, Steve, laughs, and replies

"How much you got?"

Emily is now thinking this is great. She loves the arrogant jerks as she makes so much money off them… and she thinks this is one of them.

"$50?"

Emily deliberately put it as a question to encourage his arrogance. If Emily is confident enough to suggest 50 he's likely to go higher.

"$75".

This guy clearly has no qualms about taking opposition he thinks he could beat for every penny. Not that Emily can claim moral superiority on that issue.

Emily says

"You sure?"

The guy responds "The question is are YOU sure? I could beat you one-handed if I wanted to"

Emily rolls her eyes. That's it, now she really wants to destroy him. She smiles, places her money on the side of the table and says

"Lets Play."

She ties poor Steve in knots. And she wins easily by 5 balls, even giving the guy a chance by deliberately missing a pot. The worst thing for Steve is that, before missing on purpose she told him she would miss the pot on purpose to give him a chance. She collects her winnings and walks out. Arrogant Steve mutters the word "bitch" under his breath. He had made the arrogant and sexist mistake of thinking that no girl could beat him. Had he watched the previous game, rather than just assuming that Luke must have been crap, then even arrogant Steve would have probably not gone ahead with the bet as his faulty assumption would have unravelled before his eyes.

Luke had got over his defeat and as Emily exited the bar he shouts

"Hey, you are good!"

But Emily decisively exited the bar as she had learned that it became hard to get anyone to take her on for money after she had won literally only 1 or 2 games that she had bet on. Because most people only bet when they are confident that they a comfortably the better player. Only a minority are genuinely up for a challenge.

Emily was feeling good. She walked 1 minute down the street and entered The Hard Swallow Bar. She felt thrilled as she entered the bar due to the fact that it possessed more pool tables than the average bar with tables. A guy came over to her and shamelessly hit on her.

"Hey sweetheart, fancy a drink on me?"

"I'm here to kick ass not kiss ass" declared Emily confidently as she was on a bi-polar high right now.

The guy sees Emily walk over to the pool table. She challenges another guy calle Barry to a pool game and again she's in luck as he says "yes." She deliberately plays badly again so that she loses, even playing one hell of a deliberately good shot as she pretended to carelessly pot the black to early. However, she did it on purpose. She then applies her usual tactic…

"I bet you $20 I win next time."

Barry was surprised because he didn't see anything in her performance that should have given her such confidence to bet any money.

He replied "I'm not interested in taking anyone's money."

Emily was used to this response and she was aware of what to say whenever anyone said that.

"That's ok. If you prefer if I win you pay me $20. If you win I don't pay anything."

Again, just as most do, Barry had fallen for Emily's act of being a relatively poor player and thought he will give her what she wants. And in this specific case, he's a nice guy and is grateful that an attractive female is approaching him socially. He doesn't want her to go away. So he accepts her offer. However this ended with the usual result of an Emily win. Barry was quite savvy at pool and suspected he may have been played.

"Do you always play that good?" he asked.

"No. Usually I play better" replied Emily.

"So you are a pool shark?"

"Well, actually, I consider myself a snooker shark."

"So why aren't you out destroying snooker players for money?"

"Well duh. There are bars with pool tables all over the place. Not the same for snooker."

"So you are a pool shark then, not a snooker shark."

"Nah. That's simply not true. I will win the World Championship in snooker one day."

"Wow! That's a statement. You are joking right. I mean that does sound you know ridiculous"

"Nope. The best player in the world right now is this British guy called Ronnie O' Sullivan. He made his first century break when he was 10 and his first maximum 147 break when he was 15. Well I made my first century at 9 and first 147 at 14."

"If you are telling the truth I am impressed. But I don't know if you are telling the truth or lying… or exaggerating. I mean nice coincidence that you beat him by a year on both counts."

"Oh I'm telling the truth alright." Emily pulls out a newspaper cutting that she carries around everywhere with her that reports on her 147. She shows it to Barry and then starts to walk out the bar.

"Hey where you going?"

"C ya" shouts Emily as she walks out the bar.

Emily is on a high and heads off home to her apartment. Some guy who has seen her win money in two different bars has her in his sights. He is planning on mugging her but she is in NYC's night life so there are far too many people hanging around who would definitely see him committing the crime. He needs to wait for an alleyway to appear so that he can catch up to her and before she know whats happening put his hand over her mouth and simultaneously move her into the alleyway out of sight of others eyes. The risk for the wannabe mugger is that other people will be in the alleyway. He plans to let Emily go and run for it if that is the case. Emily is half a minute or so from an Alleyway. The potential mugger starts to speed up to get closer to her. But suddenly Barry shouts to Emily

"Hey Emily!"

Barry hasn't seen the mugger. He's just after a date with the hot girl he now believes might be rich and famous one day. Emily turns round, walks right past the guy who could so easily have mugged her, says *No thanks* to Barry before flagging down a yellow cab and getting in. As she does so Barry says

"I am going to look out for you in the press you snooker shark!"

Had the mugger achieved what he had set out to do then that snooker career would have been over and Barry would have never seen or read anything about Emily ever again no matter what news media he consumed. Emily would not have been able to overcome the PTSD she would have suffered from. Many otherwise healthy people cannot cope with PTSD. PTSD for Emily would have meant that her bad days would have monopolized her life. She would have experienced complete psychological death. Barry, without knowing it, has effectively saved her already fragile mental health. Indeed, you could say that, again without knowing it, he has saved her life. Just as the mugger was going to end all hope of an American female snooker genius taking the snooker world by storm in stepped brilliant Barry to save the day. He deserved a date but Emily doesn't do dates. She doesn't even go in for friendship very much. How many American girls hang out with one-track mind snooker obsessives who want to talk and obsess solely on snooker? No wonder all of Emily's friends are male snooker players. And even they are not good enough players nor obsessive enough about snooker for Emily's liking.

Emily arrives home. She turns on the television. CNN has cut into a Program with breaking news. It is historical sensational news concerning UAP Disclosure. The first thing she hears as the television comes on is President Biden saying

"We are now in a Post-Disclosure World."

Biden has announced that UFO whistleblower David Grusch is right about exotic non human controlled crash retrievals and non-human bodies. There has indeed been a cover-up. For Emily this is all in one ear and out the other. She isn't the slightest bit interested in any of this UAP/UFO Disclosure news. The only reason she's hearing it at all is because it takes a little time to get the DVD of Ronnie O' Sullivan's 5 minutes and 8 seconds 147 on. Now its on she watches it while thinking to herself that she can get a 147 in faster time than Rocket Ronnie's 5 minutes and 8 seconds. And she longs to take his crown as the greatest snooker player that ever lived. Thus she dreams of winning the World Championship at the Crucible in Sheffield. But first, she wants to win the National U.S. Championship as everyone at the Athletic Club expected her to do so. Indeed, it is there where the U.S. Championship is held. Emily slept well tonight and indeed she would feel good tomorrow morning but the feel good factor won't last long for her.

She awoke early. She put the television on for company more than anything else. Its 24/7 UFOs. In one ear out the other as the reporter discusses what we now know in this brand new Post Disclosure World. We know for a fact, says the reporter, that the CIA's Office of Global Access Program(OGA) had played a crucial role in retrieving crashed UAP.

"Yawn Fest" says Emily to herself.

She switches the television off and phones the reigning U.S. Snooker Champion, Darren Taylor.

"Hello"

"Your going down" says Emily and then hangs up.

Taylor was well aware that only Emily Walsh would make such a call. After-all, there aren't that many female snooker players in the United States with his cell number!

Emily mutters to herself "Darren Taylor, Dennis Taylor, Fred Davis, Joe Davis, Steve Davis, Alex Higgins, John Higgins… its time that WALSH was the top name in this sport". She had rather flattered Darren Taylor by including him in that list but ideally she would like to beat him and become U.S. Champion before going on to beat the Rocket Ronnie O' Sullivan. Of course, these Snooker Tournaments could result in different outcomes. Taylor may not reach the final. Someone might knock him out in an earlier round. O' Sullivan might not make the final of the World Championship. But she was absolutely certain she would not only make the final of both competitions but also win both. At times she did think the U.S. Championship beneath her as it is a competition for amateurs but she found it insulting that her friend, Darren Taylor, is U.S. Champion when she knows for a fact that she is miles better than him as she beats him every single time she plays against him at the Athletic Club.

Emily's phone rang. It was Darren Taylor.

"Hey Emily, its me Darren, the guy you are going to take down. Anyway, I am in New York City today and meeting up with my snooker friends. Would you like to join us at Steven [Wong's] home?"

"Ok."

Later that day: Steven Wong is the beaten 2023 U.S finalist, beaten by Darren Taylor. The two come to the door and welcome Emily. Ahmed Aly Elsayed and Tom Kollins are also there… the latter two being the most successful American players in U.S. snooker's short Championship history. Nevertheless this must be the greatest informal gathering of American snooker talent ever assembled. Emily isn't so impressed. She will be more impressed with the UK's snooker family... she longs to cross the Atlantic in time for the Crucible's World Championship.

"Come in Emily"

"Hi Darren. Time for you to go down" she says heading straight for the snooker room.

"Whooaa. What's the hurry?"

"Well that's why I am here."

"She isn't the most sociable" says Tom.

Nevertheless Emily gets her way and she is soon playing snooker against Darren. They play three games and Emily wins 3–0 which included breaks of 88 and 119

They then head for the front room.

"What about that UFO news, isn't it amazing, I'm hooked" says Tom.

The guys start chatting about living in the Post-Disclosure World. They discuss what they thought about this issue as recently as the first half of the year. None of them were convinced anything exotic was going on pre Disclosure and with the exception of Aly, none of them paid any attention until just before official Presidential Disclosure. The conversation started to move onto subjective feelings of awe or uneasiness. They were trying to find out if how they felt as individuals were the same as how their friends felt. Darren kept looking over to Emily who was saying nothing. Indeed she hadn't uttered a single word since the conversation began. Then Steven started smoking DMT from a pipe. And started offering it to others.

"This will get us more into the spirit of the Post-Disclosure World." In the past that may have been said as humor. But now it was said in all seriousness.

Darren looks across at Emily again with concern. He was aware that this was not her scene. Indeed on the issue of 'scene' she was sat there reading a magazine titled 'Snooker Scene' which was not very sociable of her. Steven says

"Emily, take this. It will help you relax."

She feels pressured to conform and a moment later she is coughing and spluttering.

"Its not tobacco and too much of it will make you hallucinate" says Steven with the intention of educating a now irritated and flustered Emily.

"What the f*** has this got to do with snooker? I will answer that... a big fat NOTHING. No wonder you are all shit at the game." Emily rants.

"Ouch" says Tom at exactly the same time as Aly pleads "Emily, don't be like that."

But she storms out shouting "Losers" just before she slams the front door shut. She's angry that the only people she trusts would do things so far removed from snooker. This is an example of changed circumstances temporarily wounding her ego that craves and needs consistency and predictability.

"What a baby" says Tom.

"I don't think so" said Darren. He continues

"Just think how far removed aliens and DMT are from her world. She's neurotic for sure but we should have stuck more to snooker for her. She's not a baby, she's not psychotic. She's just a bit ill I think with Bi-polar symptoms. I'm aware she's undiagnosed though. I will call round her place tomorrow and put it right. If you treat her right she's a good person. When I call her ill I only mean fragile. That's what she is, fragile."

"I think you might understand her better than the rest of us put together" responds Aly.

Darren nods and says

"Yeah, and there's another thing I want to mention. She is worth supporting. I think she is the greatest snooker player in history. We need to help her prove it. S I am going to do some grovelling tomorrow."

Darren Taylor's opinion of Emily Walsh as the greatest snooker player in history extraordinary given that she is an 18 year old female from Brooklyn who has wor absolutely nothing yet. Indeed, it is also extraordinary for the reason that it is he that is currently the U.S. Champion, not her. But Darren has seen enough of her in action and understood that it is simply undeniable that she is world class. He approaches Emily's home, rings the door bell and notices that she is in due to seeing her through the window. But she is not answering. He peers through the letter box and shouts

"Emily. You can answer the door to me. I know you. You are smart. There's nothing wrong with you in my mind. Others think there is but I do NOT. I'm on your side. NOT theirs".

Those words worked on Emily, so she decided to answer the door and let him in.

"3–0" she said, feeling a-bit better now.

"Are you still feeling low?" replied Darren.

"No. I am the one who got the 3."

"You are going to be a star. You need someone to support you. Not just because you are young… not just because you are sensitive. Anyone would need this. People who are not stars need people. You need someone you can trust. I think you are smart. But you need to be able to open up to someone otherwise you will go wrong."

"Go wrong?"

"Yeah. I mean many people would view last night as going wrong. If that is all they see of you what do you expect them to think?"

"But you don't think that?"

"No. There's clearly something bothering you. I don't think that. What I think is that no one has listened to you and you haven't bothered explaining yourself. Maybe because you know they wouldn't listen. It's a vicious never-ending circle right? My wife thinks I am an idiot but that is because she doesn't listen to me. People who think you are an idiot just haven't listened to you."

These words of Darren's opened Emily up. She said

"When I was a child I really was a 100 per cent snooker zombie. They would have been right back then."

Darren thought for a second and then said

"But its not quite that simple now?"

"No. I mean when I was a kid I didn't know anything else so it was all obsession. But something like last night is more a defence. Of course I know about the rest of the world. Infact like you say I am quite smart but there's no point engaging."

"What do you mean, no point?"

"Well the rest of the world is idiotic."

"In what way?"

Emily goes to a draw and hands Darren something she had printed out.

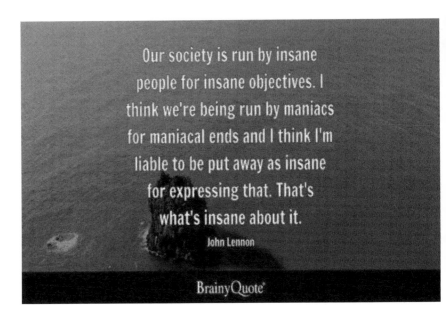

Our society is run by insane people for insane objectives. I think we're being run by maniacs for maniacal ends and I think I'm liable to be put away as insane for expressing that. That's what's insane about it.

John Lennon

BrainyQuote

Darren again pauses for a moment, reflecting. A light bulb flickers on and off his mind, as Darren starts to understand Emily a little more (albeit still far from fully) he says

"I get what you are saying. You are saying if you go along with all the manipulation, all the propaganda then you might appear sane but really you are insane given that its all about war, power, money, control and ego-mania. But you reject it then you can appear insane?"

"YES!"

Darren shakes his head…

"That might have been true in John Lennon's time, but I think most people would agree with you now. And that makes me wonder why you let it bother you?"

"People are understanding it more" says Emily. She continues "But look at this UFO stuff. It could easily be a Psy-Op yet people believe it because the most powerful have said its true. Just like people dis-believed it just because the most powerful said it was not true. If you give people power you give them the power to say what is true and false and given that power corrupts they will say what is true and false according to what is convenient for their own maintenance of their power and control. In other words, truth is not what matters to them. Their power is what matters to them. And yet people let them set the agenda for social discourse. Hence social discourse is insane."

"So this Post Disclosure World could be a way for the powerful to regain power and control?"

"Yes. That is why it was December 2017 that they came out with what they did. The likes of Trump, Brexit, and loss of faith in power is why the UFO stuff has surfaced to prominence. That is the answer to the 'Why Now?' question on Disclosure. Because by December 2017 they had decided that they were f****d if they didn't do something drastic. What can be more drastic than a UFO Psy-Op designed to rescue the powerful from losing power and control."

"So they manipulate the living shit out of the people and do Fake Disclosure."

"Exactly. Or, errmmm, probably, I'm not sure… but they can't be trusted because whatever they are saying, whether it be true or false, is for themselves. They aren't bothered about it being true. They are bothered about what they say serving themselves."

"So it pissed you off last night that we were taking it seriously?"

"Yes."

"You saw us as manipulated idiots?"

"Yes."

"Well you manipulate people so you can win money off them when you take them on at pool."

"That's fair game because they are agreeing to take money off me. They see me a female and no good so that is as much on them. Besides I am not meaning that th world be utopian. But a manipulative Propaganda Matrix that screws the people over as regularly as breathing is vile."

"Can't you just ignore it?"

"I think that is my neurosis. That is the flaw in myself. So while I think they are very flawed in one gigantic way, I accept my personal flaw. And that is the difference between the 18 year old me and 13 year old me. The 13 year old had n self-awareness. I was a snooker zombie... kinda autistic. The 18 year old me is self-aware."

"I knew it. I knew you were smart. What I don't like is that you don't defend yourself better."

"Usually when I think of 'defend' I think of people being defensive and in-denial

"Come on Emily. Ironically you give the powerful too much credit. They might b winning here and there, but most people agree with you. They have lost their power in a key way... that way being people have seen through them. It ain't the 1800s anymore."

Darren was suspicious that this was all just about the powerful duping the masses but he couldn't put his finger on it yet, so he didn't go there.

Emily says "hhmmm… what you say is relatively true but they are still able to decide whether the public accepts or rejects the existence of beyond human intelligence, i.e., non human intelligence engaging with our planet."

"Yes, it just means that they have been seen through and are getting desperate."

"It is an attempt to regain the lost authority that you refer to due to being seen through."

"Well ok, yes, but they have not won back trust outside of Disclosure."

"Oh it will be enough. People love this."

"John Lennon believed in this reality of UFO's."

Emily repeats herself somewhat by arguing

"So he did. My point isn't that UFOs/Non Human Intelligence is definitely bullshit. My point is that they may or may not be real. We don't know. My point is that the authorities tell us what is convenient for themselves. So if it is convenient to provide us with the UFO's are real narrative then they'll provide us with that narrative. If its convenient to provide us with the UFO's are bullshit narrative then they'll provide us with that narrative. The truth is irrelevant to them."

"Most people agree on the general point about the powerful, about them being in billionaires pockets and so forth."

"You keep saying that but nothing ever gets done about it."

"And what should be done about it?"

"They should lose their power. Power corrupts so we should take away excessive power. It should be illegal."

"So no more Washington DC power?"

"Right."

"When you go to the UK, they have their propaganda Matrix too... worth reminding you of that just in-case you end up living there."

"True. I know they have Westminster propaganda."

"You know you say that people don't do anything but they could say the same about you."

"Ahh, not true. I don't mean people should start a violent revolution. I mean they should know not to consume the news media and validate the politicians with votes. They say they see through it all and yet they still consume and validate that which they say they have seen through. And they are falling for it all again with UFO's because it fulfils their need for shiny mysterious discs. Anything shiny futuristic and technological goes down well with the public."

"But the public has seen through."

"Yes, but they still get played anyway. The authorities are not excessively worried about being seen through. They know to do something to counter being seen through. The public think seeing through is all they have to do. And then they continue on as before consuming and validating what they have seen through. I disagree with the public on that."

"Maybe segments of the public like this segment of the powerful but not this other segment."

"That used to be true but now almost everyone has seen through all of it. There aren't many staunch Democrats or staunch Republicans anymore. People can see those boxes are confining, limiting... and that bursting out of those boxes is freedom and unity at the same time. I don't think people are after power for themselves although if they got it it would corrupt. What I think people want is destruction of those confining boxes, without excessive ego for themselves. So you know, individuals don't walk around with an egotistical manifesto in their heads. But despite agreeing with you on all of that... What there is now is. like you say, Anti Politics, Anti Power and so on. BUT they still consume and validate it all anyway. Its like seeing through snooker and still paying money to go and watch snooker. Thus consuming and validating seen through snooker."

"Seeing through snooker... not something me or you will ever do."

"Especially me. Lets go to the Athletic Club."

"Yeah. Let's play."

3. Highs and Lows

Darren had heard enough to be sure that Emily was beyond her childhood zombie-like state and now considered her more bi-polar. She was certainly very self-aware so if autistics cannot be cured, she can't of been autistic beforehand. If autism is possible to be self-cured then maybe she had been autistic in the past.

Emily and Darren are approaching the Athletic Club when they notice six or seven club regulars mingling outside excitedly talking to someone that Emily instantly recognizes. Her face lights up as she says to Darren

"That's Mark Selby!"

"Really???"

"Yes!!! He's won the World Championship 4 times and he was runner f*****g u this year."

As they approach they catch the end of Selby explaining to the regulars that he is holidaying in New York City, doing tourist things like visiting the statue of libert going on a shopping spree, checking out central park, and splashing some of his riches on the luxury of staying at the Plaza Hotel. But he also wanted to check ou where he can play snooker and this is the place.

"Excuse me, sorry to interrupt. I'm Emily Walsh."

"Hi, Mark Selby, pleased to mee…"

"Yeah I know who you are."

"You do…"

One of the regulars thirsts to tell Mark Selby who Emily is…

"She made a 147 here aged 14."

Selby dare not believe what he just heard as he doesn't want to come across as gullible but Emily carries the proof of that around and shows Selby the newspape report.

"Wow, that happened right here". Selby is intrigued and wonders how the hell he hasn't heard of this young woman.

Emily is thirsting to kick Selby's ass right now. She is desperate. But it is Darren who speaks next.

"Hi Mark. I'm Darren Taylor, U.S. Champion."

"Right. So you aren't the U.S. Champion?" Selby says to Emily.

"Well, she almost certainly will be in a few months time when she plays in the 2024 National U.S. Championship" replies Darren on Emily's behalf.

"Delete 'Almost' responds Emily.

"She beat me 3–0 last night. In one of the frames she made a 119 break."

Selby is surprised at what he is hearing. He is fascinated, Intrigued.

"Where you from Emily?"

"Brooklyn."

"Right..." said Selby.

"Why?" asked Emily.

"Very young... female... American." Selby was embarrassed at his answer in case it came across as patronizing. But he continued...

"Doesn't add up. Doesn't compute."

Selby was thinking she can't be that good. He was thinking there's American exaggeration going on here. Selby was being rational though because since when had anywhere, never mind the U.S. where snooker is a very minor sport, produced a female capable of making a century break aged 9 and a 147 aged 14?"

Emily was now even more desperate to put Selby in his place.

"I will beat you now" she said, without a slither of joke or doubt in the tone of her voice.

The match was to be captured by multiple Athletic Club regulars recording it on their phones and uploading to Youtube. A reporter called Jennifer Rush also turne up as someone from the club phoned the press. Rush arrived just in time to witnes the start of the match and wrote a report for the New York Times about Emily Walsh's 3–1 win.

The New Y

1st November 2023

18 Year old Female Snooker

New Yorker, Emily Walsh is only 18 years old. She has never played in a professional snooker competition. But over the past 9 years she has gained quite a reputation for herself at the Athletic Club in New York City. There is where she goes to beat all-comers at snooker. It is there she made her first ever century break aged 9. It is there she made her first ever 147 maximum break aged 14. These stats alone make her a snooker genius. But now she will become known to the Brits, as she yesterday defeated 4 times world champion and 2023 runner up in the World Championship, Mark Selby 3-1 in frames. Selby is on vacation in New York. When he went to check out the Athletic Club he met Emily Walsh there. She did what she had to do. She challenged him to a few frames. The former champion accepted. Walsh went 2-0 up within 25 minutes, making a 133 break in the second frame. Selby hit back in the third frame winning it 76-67 in a true nail-biter. But then in what the two decided would be the final frame, Walsh won 91-2

Rush wrote the following… *New Yorker, Emily Walsh is only 18 years old. She has never played in a professional snooker competition. But over the past 9 years*

she has gained quite a reputation for herself at the Athletic Club in New York City.
There is where she goes to beat all-comers at snooker. It is there she made her first
ever century break aged 9. It is there she made her first ever 147 maximum break
aged 14. These stats alone make her a snooker genius. But now she will become
known to the Brits, as she yesterday defeated 4 times world champion and 2023
runner up in the World Championship, Mark Selby 3–1 in frames. Selby is on
vacation in New York.When he went to check out the Athletic Club he met Emily
Walsh there. She did what she had to do. She challenged him to a few frames. The
former champion accepted. Walsh went 2–0 up within 25 minutes, making a 133
break in the second frame. Selby hit back in the third frame winning it 76–67 in a
true nail-biter. But then in what the two decided would be the final frame, Walsh
won 91–2.

After the Selby match the reporter offered Emily a 4pm tomorrow interview at the
New York Times. She accepted the invitation.

Emily couldn't wait and all her worries about the world had melted away. On the
contrary to being worried, she was on her highest ever bi-polar high. It was just 2
hours before the interview with Rush and she was doing something she had never
done before… drinking wine. (Chardonnay to be precise). It didn't take much for
Emily to get drunk. But she was enjoying the combination of her highest ever bi-
polar high combined with being merrily drunk. She turns up for the interview with
Rush.

Rush: Hi Emily, congrats on your win over Mark Selby. So are you two in touch
now? Do you have his mobile number?

Emily: No. I wouldn't mind yours though.

Rush: You wouldn't mind my number? Why's that? I am no snooker player.

Emily: You are hot sweetheart. That's why.

Rush: Have you been drinking?

Emily walks over to the reporter, puts an arm behind the reporters neck, pushes it forward, and kisses her on the lips. Rush backs off Emily and says this interview over.

Emily: "Wow! That was worth it" she says giggling as she leaves the scene.

Unfortunately for Emily, Jennifer Rush tells others at the New York Times what happened and they run a story on the incident carrying the headline 'Emily Walsh not such a Goody two shoes'.

The New Y

3rd November 2023

Emily Walsh not such a Goo

New York Snooker Sensation, 18 year old Emily Walsh is known for her single-minded focus on her sport. She has seemingly sacrificed the lure of alcohol, boyfriends and even friends. But wait, is that true? Yesterday an interview with our very own Jennifer Rush had to be cancelled when the teen star hit on our reporter, even landing a kiss on her lips. She was intoxicated with alcohol and in no state to go ahead with the interview. Is Walsh in decline already

despite only two days ago beating the former world champion, Mark Selby at the Athletic Club in New York City? She has certainly made a name for herself beyond snooker here at the Times. She may need to lay off the alcohol as she will not be making those century breaks if her vision is blurred. Our advice to the snooker star is to get back to what you do best... dedicating yourself to snooker otherwise your career is going to be over before its even begun.

The NYT Report: New York Snooker Sensation, 18 year old Emily Walsh is known for her single-minded focus on her sport. She has seemingly sacrificed the lure of alcohol, boyfriends and even friends. But wait, is that true? Yesterday an interview with our very own Jennifer Rush had to be cancelled when the teen star hit on our reporter, even landing a kiss on her lips. She was intoxicated with alcohol and in no state to go ahead with the interview. Is Walsh in decline already despite only two days ago beating the former world champion, Mark Selby at the Athletic Club in New York City? She has certainly made a name for herself beyond snooker here at the Times. She may need to lay off the alcohol as she will not be making those century breaks if her vision is blurred. Our advice to the snooker star is to get back to what you do best... dedicating yourself to snooker otherwise your career is going to be over before its even begun.

The bad news did not end there for Emily. She had a new found reputation in the UK as a snooker genius following the win over Selby. But the news media also picked up on this New York Times incident involving reporter Rush. Several UK news media outlets covered the story including ITV News who picked up on the New York Times *Goody Two Shoes* headline and thus played the Adam Ant song throughout their 4 minute report.

Darren Taylor was gutted for Emily. He thought that she had got carried away like someone who goes from being a non-gambler to an addict because of winning a few one off bets that were really just beginneers luck wins. They then throw all their money away as they end up chasing their losses. Well Emily had that adreneline rush in terms of what she perceived as social glory. All her life she had felt socially anxious and isolated... and thus she got carried away fueled by her bi-polar and wine. But now she had metaphorically-speaking lost a fortune. Given Emily's mental health condition she had experienced a severe collapse.

Darren calls round at her Brooklyn home.

"Emily, don't worry. That wasn't the real you. You just need to get used to the social world so you become more socially savvy. You have dived right into the deep end of the swimming pool having never done much more than dipped your toes in the shallow end."

Emily doesn't say anything. She stares at Darren intensely. This looks bad. Almo a minute passes and she's still not said anything and Darren notices that she is physically shaking. And he notices the fear in Emily's face.

"Emily, say something. You are scaring me."

"I have done something stupid."

Now Darren's heart is racing.

"What…. what… what have you done?"

Tears well up in Emily's eyes. She glances over to what looks like empty paracetamol packets.

"Jesus Christ!!!!!" Now Darren's hands are shaking. Emily slips into unconsciousness. He makes the inevitable call.

"911 what's your emergency?"

4. The Hendry/Walsh Interview

10 weeks later

The catastrophic attempt to take her own life nearly worked. She had received 8 weeks of hospital care and two weeks of pampering from her small group of friends in the American snooker family. The news media had only just started to build her up and shoot her down but had already gone quiet concerning Emily. You could say that the news media were rather bi-polar themselves concerning their attitude to Emily Walsh. They were intrigued by her but they also understood that they were in the firing line for having nearly been the cause of her committing suicide.

British Sky Sports News had promised her a gentle interview that would stick 99% to snooker and ask nothing personal beyond how are you feeling now? Emily was decisively going to turn them down until they said that Stephen Hendry would conduct the interview. That made her decisively say "Yes". So she flew over to London, and nobody would be able to stop her.

The Hendry/Walsh Interview:

Hendry: Hi Emily. I have heard a-lot about you.

Walsh: I've heard a lot about you too.

Hendry: Given that you have flew over to the UK I am guessing you are recovered from your attempt on your own life?

Walsh: Yes.

Hendry: You want to move straight onto the snooker don't you?

Walsh: [nods]

Hendry: I have always said that Ronnie O' Sullivan is the best/most naturally talented snooker player ever. What is your response to that?

Walsh: He is the second best.

Hendry: [Smiling] So I am the b...

Walsh: [laughing/interuptting] I see where you are going there. No, you are third.

Hendry: Ok. You are very forward when it comes to snooker. Shall we say confident. Talk to me about Ronnie and you in terms of similarities and differences.

Walsh: Well Ronnie plays as good as me when he's in the mood. When he is not the mood he collapses. Now I am undiagnosed bi-polar but when I play snooker that lifts me. My mood is always outstanding if I regard it as a competitive match Being American I haven't actually played a match that is officially competitive. So I mean 'competitive' in my subjective unofficial kinda way. Snooker focuses my mind. I do not think that is always the case with Ronnie.

Hendry: But what if you were going through a down before a match?

Walsh: If it were severe I would be a no-show. But sometimes my down's are exaggerations and I just need the snooker drug to lift me to a high that focuses my mind. Then I am in the zone.

Hendry: Ronnie, once conceded a match against me when he had no-where near lost. I was amazed.

Walsh: Yeah. I have seen that. I would be on a high if I had been playing in that match against you. That wouldn't happen with me.

Hendry: Can you say more on how it is that you don't experience a down in snooker?

Walsh: Because I think I am focusing on what matters. In other words, snooker is what matters. So it dissociates the other problems. The other issues become insignificant... until they resurface again later when I am not in the snooker bubble.

Hendry: I do see great similarities though with you and Ronnie. Ronnie's dad was sentenced to 17 years in prison when Ronnie was only 16. For murder. His story is dramatic as well.

Walsh: Yeah, I watched a documentary on Ronnie that made me aware of that. You will know what I am on about... *'Ronnie O' Sullivan: Edge of Everything'* and his mother didn't initially tell the 16 year old Ronnie about the sentence because she wanted him to focus on his snooker. I have watched that documentary about 5 times.

Hendry: It's only been available to watch for a few months! Anyway, what makes you a better player than Ronnie though? So let me think... you are saying that he can be as good as ...

Walsh: [Interrupting]... You know when Ronnie is at his best getting say, a 130 break...

Hendry: [Interrupting]... Yeah, he makes those century breaks more than anyone.

Walsh: No he doesn't. I make them one every 2 or 3 frames.

Hendry: Wow. Wow. So just to speak to the viewers for a moment. Remember th person I am talking to here is, how old are you again 18 or 19 [Walsh says 19 in few weeks] and she is saying that despite her youth, her American nationality, an being female, because lets face it, this isn't a big sport among American men, never mind American women... but she is saying that she is more naturally talented than Ronnie O' Sullivan. [Hendry returns his focus to Walsh, looks at he and says...] That's ok. I am enjoying this. I can't wait to see you playing in this year's World Championship. You are already a celebrity in the UK. Are you a celebrity in the United States?

Walsh: I am in New York.

Hendry: You are going to make snooker bigger here in the UK than it was at its peak in the 1980's. People here are fascinated by you. And you know, you could single-handedly make snooker as big as football... ermmm, soccer.

Walsh: Yeah, that's what Mark Selby said to me as well. He predicted it based o the British people's love of an underdog with me being young, female, American

Hendry: And although we won't go deep into it, your attempt on your life as wel adds to the interest in you.

Walsh: This interview is going a lot better than my last one.

Hendry: There is one thing other thing going on in the world that is receiving a-l of attention... the UFO Post Disclosure World. What do you think about that?

Walsh: Nothing.

Hendry: Really, nothing?

Walsh: Nothing.

[a moments awkward silence]

Hendry: Ok, back to the snooker.

Walsh: Look you can't trust those with those messages. They play people. That's why I say nothing.

Hendry: So what's next for you? Because the World Championship is 3 months away at the moment.

Walsh: The U.S. National Championship.

Hendry: Oh yes, and its actually played at the same venue that you have been playing in since you were a girl.

Walsh: Yes, the Athletic Club in New York City.

Hendry: I don't suppose there is anyone there who can compete against you? Well obviously not.

Walsh: That's right. Obviously not. My friend Darren Taylor is ok. He is about as good as someone who would go out in the first round at the Crucible.

Hendry: Put some big glasses on his face and call him Dennis.

Walsh: And get him to raise his snooker cue above his head and act like he has just won the World Championship against Steve Davis. And then tell him that's as close as he will get to actually doing that. [Tears start to pour down Emily's face as she says] He saved my life. If he hadn't called round when he did I would have died.

Hendry passes Emily a tissue and she composes herself. She smiles and says...

but I'm alright right now. Right where I want to be.

Hendry: You know that if you are as good as you think you are, and I think you very well might be, that you will have to travel to places other than the UK… for example, to Asia for competitions. Are you happy to do that?

Walsh: For snooker, definitely.

Hendry: Snooker is no longer a man's world.

Walsh: There are plenty of women who are good at pool in the U.S. and I think that is the case here in Britain too. But yeah, glass ceiling smashing time.

Hendry: Many people out there do think you must be over-rated though.

Then Emily hears a cockney accent in the background… singing ABBA's *Money Money Money.*

If I had a little money, it's a rich man's world.

Hendry: Come in Ronnie. Meet your match.

Walsh: Oh my God!!!!! My hero!!!!! [She had just wiped tears away with a tissue But now tears of happiness well up in Emily's eyes as she meets Ronnie O' Sullivan].

O' Sullivan: I'm not sure I feel the same way about you given how often I hear ye say you are even more naturally gifted at snooker than I am.

Walsh: Well, errmm, yeah. But… you are a legend. You know, I want to beat you 5 minute 8 second 147. That's the one thing that I don't think I have done.

O' Sullivan: How would you know? I mean, you don't time your practise games right?

Walsh: Actually I do in-case I beat that 147 time.

Hendry: Wow, Wow, Wow. You actually time your snooker games just in-case you get a 147 maximum in faster time than 5 minutes and 8 seconds. I never thought I would even hear that said.

Walsh: I got 5 minutes 12 seconds about a year ago.

O' Sullivan: Slow Coach.

Walsh: I didn't think about speeding up until a little of the way through the break.

Hendry: Ok guys, I think we need to wrap this up. But it has been fascinating. I would do interviews all the time if they were always like this one. But now I am being told to go to a commercial break and when we return it will be back to the studio with some big breaking football news.

Emily exited the building with Ronnie O' Sullivan.

"So what are you doing now?" Emily asked the Rocket as she craved a game of snooker against him.

"I've got a Mental Health charity event to go to."

Ronnie was about to ask Emily what she is going to do now when a fan shouted

"RONNIE, RONNIE"

The fan approached the pair, and asked for O' Sullivan's autograph. He obliged, The fan then said...

"You are that American, Emily Walsh?"

"Yup"

"Can I have your autograph please?"

Emily signed her name for the fan.

"And so it starts"… said the Rocket smiling at Emily.

"Anyway" Ronnie continued, "I must be getting to the event. Take care Emily."

As Ronnie walked away Emily half jokingly shouted

"RONNIE!"

Ronnie looks back at Emily who shouts

"Your going down!"

Ronnie laughed and walked on. She wondered if it were a bit strange not to open up to him on mental health as Ronnie is clearly a Mental Health advocate and ope on the issue. But she was here for the snooker. And besides she felt better than ev today despite not getting to take Ronnie on at snooker. She would never forget meeting Stephen Hendry and Ronnie O' Sullivan for the first time. She would discuss her mental health progress with Darren when she gets back to Brooklyn.

5. Rebirth

Darren is at Emily's Brooklyn apartment again. It would be understandable for people to start to wonder if they are going to start dating. But that is not on either Darren's or Emily's mind. People see them together so much that they assume Darren is single. But he is married.

Darren is delighted that Emily's trip to the UK went so amazingly well.

"You know Emily, I think a lot of your negative emotion aimed at the powerful is projection."

Emily wonders about that view. A year ago it would have triggered her. She responds

"Much of it, yes. But not all. After-all, the system is presided over by the powerful for their own benefit and against the poor's interests even as they pretend to be on the poor's side. But I think the negative emotion part of it is projection."

"You mean the part that actually makes you feel triggered is itself the part that you are projecting?"

"Yes. I think we need to be together against the system but we must not exaggera how amazingly moral we are by getting all hot under the collar with negative emotion. I mean, we would be the same if we were in power. Since when does anyone give power up voluntarily? This is a brain issue, we are right about what our brain tells us is going on… the powerful ruling for themselves and their mate But when we get all broken hearted about it that is us playing their manipulative game. They don't have sleepless nights about their corruption and we don't have sleepless nights about their corruption."

"But you don't mean that as a get out of jail for free card for the ruling class?"

"No. That would be to normalize corruption."

"Errmm…"

"Yeah, I know what you are thinking. It is normalized. But that doesn't mean I should normalize it."

"It's a difficult balance then isn't it" pondered Darren. You are trying to speak truth to power without getting emotionally involved."

"Yeah. The point is not to obsess about it."

"Right. Obsession is for snooker?"

"Yes. I can't get outside of myself to be objective about snooker."

"Your mental illness then…. do you think as a child it was autism?"

"I think I was repressing life because I couldn't make sense of it. Look if its impossible to be cured from autism then I can't have been autistic. Because I hav become more self-aware. When I was a child I suspected much of the world as a sham. Now I know what it was I was suspecting of being a sham."

"But that repressing of life is not to be recommended?"

"That's true!"

"But you still have bi-polar ups and downs?"

"Right. So I figure that to make sense of life, to bring order to life, we have to put the individual ego in it's place. That is what I have had to do. So let's take myself as an example. There's an habitual stimulus-response to what I think is fake news. This could be on pop culture. It doesn't have to be in relation to ruling class stuff." [This interested Darren as he had suspected that there was more to her neurosis than she had discussed. He had already got an emotion confession out of Emily and now she was discussing wider society issues in relation to mental health. Emily was however, aware, of her diverging from the ruling class issue]. "Indeed," continued Emily, "its a better example to use pop culture because the Propaganda Matrix is set up to manipulate the public thus everything is distorted. Its slanted and biased towards the powerful's interests by design. The Propaganda Matrix is a special case. But with pop culture its not a special case and therefore is a better example. So there's all kinds of individual ego bias nonsense in life and the problem with that is it makes authentic relating an impossibility. Because when someone is like that then the other person is just talking to him or herself. All he or she is doing is identifying with their own bullshit. Its fine to possess an individual perspective or an individual taste. We all have an ego. But where it goes wrong is when it denies the collective taste. I am using the word 'taste' because this is about pop culture. So for example its fine to like 'When Harry met Sally' as one's favourite film but don't claim its bigger than 'Star Wars'. Far more people put Star Wars top. Studies and polls show this to be the case. Ditto it's fine to think Michael Buble is the coolest music artist ever but again studies show that the likes of Queen, the Beatles, and the Rolling Stones are the coolest. The individual can

41

only possess a myth that its different. Are we speaking individually or collectively? Not everyone thinks their tastes are the biggest or the best. In-fact the study I have in-mind shows that 52% of people think their music taste is NOT cool."

Emily shows Darren some of the studies/polls.

"Some of these studies are British, the music one entirely so." says Darren while wondering if the pop culture issue really matters.

"Ahh, yes, that's deliberate. I will explain why in a moment."

Darren is intrigued but as she said "in a moment" he figures he can wait.

"But your bi-polar symptoms mean you DO react to things you see and hear?"

"This Individual — Collective perspective is my attempt at cure. I have just recently come up with the idea."

"I think the individual would need to be seen routinely as subordinate to the stronger collective otherwise you would drift into old bad habits. Bad habits die hard."

"Yes. The collective brain is a good brain. The individual brain is biased, slanted, lacks objectivity because it allows emotional nonsense to over-ride it. If you view the collective intellectually then you can't dissociate or collapse because you are not emotionally invested in anything. Its emotional involvement that leads us astray. Emotional involvement makes liars of us all. It messes us up as well. Ronnie O; Sullivan once conceded an entire match against Hendry because he was too emotionally involved when he had nowhere near been defeated."

"4 minutes and 24 seconds."

"What is 4 minutes and 24 seconds? One of my century breaks?"

"No. How long you went without talking about snooker."

"Oh right. I should have given you a gift I just received."

"Another gift I don't know about."

"Yup."

"I still don't quite get how you can talk about order in the mind, while you are so obsessed with snooker?"

"Look, I am too involved with snooker, I admit it. I can't take an objective outside look at it when I am immersed in it myself. But I am a special case because my obsession benefits me. How rare is that? What I mean is 99.99999% of people with an obsession do not gain out of it. They are far more likely to mentally collapse because of it. It's not healthy."

Darren could not put his finger on Emily's condition but thought that she showed signs of being every bit as self aware as he is, and smarter, while still being too strident about things that he was totally unaware she considered to be important.

"I'm intrigued about your improvement in mental health. How have you done it?" asks Darren pouring a couple of glasses of wine. Emily is no longer tee-total and there's no risk of her becoming alcoholic as she cannot stand the hangover experience which she experienced once following the Jennifer Rush interview.

"The suicide attempt was one hell of a wake-up call. I have never done so much self-reflection in my life. The urgency feeling made me think a-lot. What felt impossible to do in the past felt much easier due to the shock to my system. My fear was beyond words"

"You don't seem to have PTSD?"

"It feels more like rebirth."

Emily continues…

"I just need success, independence, arms length relationships meaning boundaries because otherwise I always feel like I have to do other people's psychology for them and check myself for potential hypocrisy. It's never ending."

"I see. Anyway, moving on… so you were mentioning gifts?"

"Well before I get to the gifts for me and you… eerrr, don't get excited, mainly gifts for me, not so much for you, I just want to say that I am being a giver as well I think we could prove a collective knowledge truth that snooker is not big culturally in NYC or the U.S. in general. And on snooker not being part of popular culture here in NY, I am helping with that. I think I am mainstreaming snooker here in NY and like was said in my Hendry interview, making it bigger than it ever was in the 80s in the UK. You know about 1 in 3 British people watched the 1985 Davis/Taylor final."

"My cousin won that final."

"Ha ha, very funny. Here, the news about the gifts you are craving to hear about. Stephen Hendry gave me two gifts to bring back to New York with me… one was these giant glasses for you to wear so we can call you Dennis Taylor."

He puts the giant glasses on, and looks in the mirror.

"I would need a wig to look like Dennis. And as for being called Dennis, I am rather attached to my Darren Taylor name. But I am happy with Darren Dennis Taylor. So tell me, what was Hendry's second gift to you?"

"A stop-watch."

"A stop-watch???"

"Yes. For accurately timing my 147 breaks so I will know to the second if I have beaten Rocket Ronnie's 5 minutes 8 seconds fastest ever 147. And Ronnie gave me a gift too."

"What would that be? Did he provide the wig?"

"Nah. Well it isn't just Ronnie. Rather the snooker family over in the UK chipped in to buy me a house in the UK. They know I will be able to pay them back before long although I'm not sure whether or not they are asking for that. Probably depends how quickly I get success. But I'm not leaving New York yet. I have the U.S. National Championship coming up first. That is why I fact-checked, specifically-speaking, the UK's collective tastes as I think I will probably spend the rest of my life living in the UK."

"That is amazing. Its obvious that you are part and parcel of the snooker family now. I will miss you when you leave though. This calls for another wine and some music to celebrate."

"Oh I still love this city so put this on…" 1 minute later Sinatra's *New York* is blasting out at full volume.

"Arghh"

"What is it?" asks Emily.

"Check this out" Darren says to Emily as he turns up the television volume and turns down the Sinatra volume.

The CNN news reporter is saying Anti State riots have broken out in New York City with people angry that they were lied to about the nature of reality (UFOs, Non-Human Intelligence) for 80 years.

45

"Sounds like a good time to be leaving."

"Except you are not leaving yet. We cursed it, playing *New York* and you saying how much you loved New York."

"You'll visit me in England right?" replied Emily who clearly didn't foresee the consequences for her of these riots.

"You bet ya. I will be at the crucible."

"You sure you can get a ticket?"

"With you as my friend and with your contacts, I would be amazed if that proved to be a problem."

"Good point."

"You saved my life Darren."

"No problem. After the Championship here you'll get on that plane to the UK and prove to the world that you are the greatest snooker player of all-time."

"Some people think it must all be exaggeration because I am American, 18 and female."

"That is what makes you so amazing. Its not exaggeration. So like I just said, go out and prove it."

The U.S. Snooker Championship was just 10 days away. But all anyone in New York City is talking about was the riots that had engulfed the city as angry anti establishment protesters and rioters cause chaos day after day. They are simply angry that for approximately 80 years the State had kept their knowledge of Non Human Intelligence engaging earth covered up. Emily thinks that there is a lie on one side or the other. Either the 80 year cover up where the authorities said this is all nonsense was a lie or they are lying now about this all being real. What is for sure is that most people accepted the new reality. But it isn't just the historical and cosmic lie about NHI that bothers people. It is that this sealed the ruling classes fate. There is nothing they won't lie about, no corruption that is too much for them. They are only coming clean to try and restore trust in the State... but that has backfired. But things got even worse. In this Post-Disclosure World much power had shifted from the old Ruling Class to the UFO Researchers that had got so much right. And power had gone to at least one researchers head already as he kept informing the news media that the extraterrestrials may well be unfriendly. Worse, he said, we may have gone and broken an agreement with them not to disclose their existence. These comments had everyday life consequences for New Yorkers already suffering from the worst riots in the cities history. The comments added fear to anger and that meant while thousands protested and rioted, thousands more tried to flee the city. Then, for Emily, things got really bad. The U.S. Snooker Championship was cancelled due to players being unwilling to go to New York City as NY was now a no-go area for Americans. People wanted to leave as opposed to get in. This was due to the riots and because of that New Yorker view of themselves as the target of enemies. Many people not from NY agreed that the famous city was a target for enemies. In this case the enemies being extraterrestrial. Emily was gutted. She thought it a good thing that people had seen through the old ruling class... who are no longer the ruling class. But she was gutted that they had (without them even realising it) replaced that old corrupt ruling class with UFO Researchers. Nothing has really changed... people were right to get rid of power. Wrong to replace it with power. The result in Emily's view was the continuation of excessive power and influence. The old order was responsible for the anger and thus the riots. The new order is responsible for the fear and thus the fleeing of NYC. But it is not so easy to just leave the country.

And this is a real problem for Emily. She's already going to miss the U.S. Championship at the start of February 2024. And potentially worse… if she cannot get to the UK by the end of February she will miss a BBC Pot Black Charity event being arranged for entertainment and charitable reasons by Ronnie O' Sullivan with Emily Walsh billed as the figure people will be tuning in to watch. She is gaining more and more fans in the UK. The cancellation of the U.S. Championship had no bearing on her professional status. But there is a lot of people wanting to see her on television in Britain and she is yearning to placate them. After-all, she is all for making snooker bigger, and herself, big in the UK.

Emily is now feeling anxious but she does receive a phone call from the Athletic Club that improves her mood. The phone call consists a-lot of comments such as "I'm sorry" about the cancellation of the tournament. And much "its not your fault" type comments from Emily. But there's also something that made Emily feel better. She is informed that the Athletic Club is going to change its name to 'THE EMILY WALSH SNOOKER CLUB'. That put a smile on Emily's face.

6. War of the Worlds

Emily, now 19 is stuck in New York City. No U.S. Championship was played this year. The late February/early March 2024 Pot Black Event was played without the star attraction being present. And she was not as much in the limelight as she hoped. She did a few online interviews with UK and NY media so she no longer had to kick ass at pool in NY bars everyday. And of course the re-naming of the Athletic Club was a proud moment. But the violent and fearful post-disclosure world was inescapable… quite literally inescapable for Emily Walsh and many others. She wasn't afraid of course. She wasn't fearing a War of the Worlds scene But most others did want escape due to fear. If the word 'afraid' meant anything to

Emily it would be about Emily being afraid of missing the World Championship at the Crucible in Sheffield which starts on 20 April 2024.

Emily feels trapped inside her house most of the time. That never used to be perceived as a problem when she was a little younger as she used to be isolated from the world. Now she wants out of not only her house, but also her city and her country. She switches on the TV and looks at the listings schedule. It's almost 24/7 Post Disclosure World Documentaries. There may be a Psy-Op going on here she thought to herself. But she isn't sure. Far from it. She couldn't apply a collective taste study to this because she regarded the UFO issue as tied to the Propaganda Matrix thus the people are manipulated and frequently brainwashed one way or the other. Emily muttered 'violent sheep' to herself when she glanced at a screen of rioters… sheep they may be but they were powerful enough to prevent her from catching a plane out of here. Emily thought that the only way we could make sense of the UFO issue would be if no manipulative Propaganda Matrix existed. Then we would simply be able to ask the perfectly honest State what the truth is and we would all be able to accept the answer. But in reality we know they lie because the State has changed its position on UFO's just like they have for decades changed their story again and again on Roswell, each time expecting us to believe what they are saying this time despite their 0% score so far concerning telling the truth in the past. Emily thought there is probably a lie going on here as well but the people preferred this lie. Well that WAS the case. But then a UFO researcher said that the ETs may be unfriendly. Now many people want to be told the old lie again. But the genie is out the bottle. And it was threatening to bring down New York City. But If it brings down New York City it will spread and bring about the end of the United States of America.

Emily's mind swung back to her way of thinking... the way she must think to ensure that her bi-polar mind doesn't kill her. Remember it wasn't that long ago that she attempted to kill herself. So she scribbled down on a note:

I can like X. That is individual.

But my individual like of X does not mean that the collective has the same position

It is only when emotional identification demands that the individual ego and the collective be one-and-the-same that we go wrong.

So understand the difference. i.e., there is individual truth and there is collective truth.

Emily was also policing others ego's in the sense of using this obvious system to understand when others were making this mistake. After-all, she pondered, why should any of us conform to others emotional biases. We apply the brain to their errors. So we should do so to our own errors. Darren now thought that Emily over thinks. That being said, Emily's individual/collective logic is how many healthy people automatically think. So Darren was still unsure what to make of Emily and this is despite thinking that he understands her better than anyone else.

But her new found way of thinking was not helping concerning the riots preventing her catching a plane to London. So she immersed herself in old copies of *Snooker Scene* Magazine. And she watched the Ronnie O' Sullivan documentary again. Sh thought that whatever the diagnosis for Ronnie's condition, he was certainly bi-polar within the snooker context. She thought she could beat Ronnie of course because she played like Ronnie at his best. Moreover when on a snooker table she possessed the mental focus of Stephen Hendry at his best. She considered Ronnie mentally up and down at the table. She both considered him her hero and also considered him second to herself. Locked in to her Brooklyn home she craved taking the crown off the Rocket. She wanted him to be firmly considered the second most naturally talented player of all time. Just like he had taken the crown off Stephen Hendry. Just like Hendry had taken the crown off Steve Davis. Only this time no-one would ever take the crown off Emily Walsh.

Emily was still making sports news herself. The U.S. Snooker Championship had made more news than ever before in it's history thanks to her. And this despite it's cancellation. And the UK Sports news had her no-show for the Pot Black Mental Health Charity event as making as much sports headlines as if it were a shock postponing of a huge Champions League football match involving an English team following their team being injured in a coach crash. She had passionate fans in the UK who saw her as a hero. They were a new type of snooker fan (more akin to the noise level of tennis fans cheering on a Brit at Wimbledon) who might be required to become more quiet if they ever get to see their hero at the Crucible.

Emily, who usually avoided the news shows like the plague was now switching onto those same news programs desperate to see a fizzling out of the panic stricken New Yorkers overwhelming the New York City airlines.

In the meantime Emily was delighted that Darren Taylor would be joining her, assuming they get out of New York in time, at the Crucible as he had attained professional status and would compete in the first round. And by coincidence when the draw was made Taylor was drawn against Mark Selby, who Emily had beaten easily at the Athletic Club. When Emily next met up with Darren in a coffee shop away from the rioters, she said to him

"Lol, you are going to get slaughtered."

Meanwhile Emily herself had been drawn against John Higgins in the First round.

Throughout March people in New York stopped believing in an Apocalypse style War of the Worlds attack on their city simply because it hadn't happened. The UFO researcher who had triggered the panic was never listened to again, his reputation in tatters. Other UFO researchers were a little more careful realizing their new found power was real.

Emily received an invite from ITV's Good Morning Britain (GMB) and the monetary offer for accepting the interview blew her mind. Let's just say it made her rich overnight. She was already offering to pay back money for her new Sheffield home.

The extraterrestrials had been a no-show. Emily Walsh was not surprised in the slightest. She was overjoyed. That meant that she could now get a flight to the UK. She and Darren Taylor left the U.S. together, Emily for good, Darren temporarily. She would NOT be a no-show for the 5th April GMB interview.

7. Emily Walsh in the UK

On the morning of Emily Walsh's GMB interview she arrived at ITV Studio's and instantly understood her fame and popularity in this country. Hundreds of fans had crowded outside the building and when she arrived they chanted "EMILY EMILY EMILY" and despite being Brits they waved U.S. flags to welcome their hero. She had to sign countless autographs. And she had never won a trophy yet!

Hazel Irvine, who presents the Snooker World Championship for the BBC every year would be the Emily Walsh interviewer, this despite it being a live ITV interview.

The interview went very well. The only worry Emily had was that Irvine would refer to the Jennifer Rush interview, but the interviewer was sensible and kind enough to avoid that, focusing her questions on her recovery instead. These were kind questions because it gave Emily the chance to give honest and positive answers based on feeling reborn rather than feeling like a psychological mess. Moreover, it gave Emily the chance to say that her mental health is transformed for the better from what it was just a year ago. And it gave her the chance to say she is keen on ideas such as the Pot Black/Mental Health charity event that she was unable to be at. Naturally there were also questions about the Post Disclosure World. Emily didn't really want to get into that. There was discussion about Darren Taylor who Emily admitted she thought would go out in the first round.

"That's your friend" responded Irvine. But Emily was simply being honest and realistic.

When Irvine asked if she might become more than just good friends with Taylor, Emily replied she was married to snooker and that Darren was married to his wife.

"Ouch!" responded Irvine. "There will be a lot of disappointed fans."

"Why? Is Darren that popular?"

"No, I mean because you are married to snooker" replied Irvine laughing.

One of those disappointed fans might have been better described as an obsessive stalker languishing outside, mingling in with the less criminally inclined fans. She got a taxi home and the stalker got in his car and stealthily followed her.

Now he knows where she lives.

The next morning, bright and early at about 6.30 Emily was out on a run. She had been influenced by Ronnie O' Sullivan who runs for the sake of his mental health. Her Stalker see's her leave her house and start running. The obsessive man has binoculars and allows her to get some way in the distance before starting the engine of his car. He starts to follow. Emily is pushing herself. She is no slouch. But this means that when she tripped it hurt more than if she were a slouch. She tripped on uneven pavement and she hit the deck and grazed her knee which started bleeding. She felt the horrible pain but was relieved that her hands were merely a little sore from their failed attempt to provide herself with a safe landing Suddenly her stalker rushed towards her. He pretended not to recognise her. He helped Emily to her feet. She felt a sharp sensation as he did so and that surprised her a-little as she had not felt pain in that part of her body when she hit the concrete. And she also had a limp due to her injured knee. He told Emily it's her lucky day as he is a doctor, which of course was a lie. He asked where she lived despite knowing where she lives. And he asks how long she has lived there despit knowing that she has only just arrived. When she said she had just moved in, he told her that she would need a local friend as he lives only 10 minutes walk away Or 30 minutes away for limpers. He helped her back to her door. Astonishingly he resisted asking to come in. This was clever of the stalker because he thought that she would feel like inviting him in as that would be the decent thing for her to do. And she did. He of course, accepted the invite.

Emily Walsh had been kidnapped.

The Stalkers name was Eddie Wilkinson. On entering Emily's home he immediately asked about Darren Taylor. This made no sense to Emily as only a few minutes ago he had acted like he didn't know who she was. That made her frightened and scared of what his intentions were.

"Are you really a doctor?"

"I'm your number 1 fan."

"Well, I'm not with Darren in that way... but we are friends and he will be calling around later on. Soon in fact."

"Oh we don't want him disturbing us."

That made Emily panic even more. Emily wondered how violent this guy would be willing to be. Because he already sounds obsessed to her. He's mad but she had no idea how much force he would be willing to use against her, if any.

"Well you know that I am friends with the snooker world here in the UK... well they know where I live. Someone famous could call round. And you know what the press are like. A-bit like you really, ha" said Emily, pretending to find some humor in the predicament she found herself in.

"I'm going to let you go."

"Oh thank god" said Emily, instantly regretting showing the kidnapper that she didn't trust him.

"Well you need to win the World Championship."

"Right."

"So we only have a fortnight together."

"You can't stay here til 20th April. Are you crazy?"

Wilkinson started to think about how to do this. Emily tried to persuade him of the insanity of what she now understood as a kidnapping. And she appealed to any conscience he may possess.

"You know a lot about me right?"

"Yes."

"So you know I have suffered psychologically. Do you care about me?"

"Of course I do!"

"So how do you think this helps my mental health?"

Wilkinson went quiet again… again clearly thinking about what it is he wants to do or at least pretending to give off that impression. Emily started to think he had no plan. She theorized he is not only mad but also hopefully and probably, naive Emily had a plan of her own. She was thinking if he is very naive he will keep her kidnapped here. She therefore regretted saying that people may call round. It was relatively true. She was certain that Darren would call at some point. But she thought it would sound suspicious if she suddenly started offering him tea or coffee. So she tried a different strategy,

"There's only one way I know how to relax in stressful situations" Emily said to Wilkinson. "And that is to play snooker. I challenge you to a few frames."

This made Wilkinson ecstatic. This was the madman's dream come true. Well that is what he said anyway. He accepted.

"Are you any good?" asked Emily.

"My highest break is 42."

Emily wanted to maintain his trust. So she was polite as she could be..

"How do you want me to play against you?"

"What do you mean?"

"Well do I play like I would in the World Championship or do I give you a ton of chances?"

"hhmmm…"

"I tell you what… I will play the first game like it is a World Championship game then you can decide how I play in the second game."

"Deal."

At 8am with this farce of a snooker match still continuing, Emily's mobile rang. It was Darren. Wilkinson suddenly turned aggressive in terms of sternly warning Emily to tell him that he shouldn't come round today because she is feeling sick. But Emily used her brain and when the call ended, which she incidentally ended it slightly oddly abruptly (in order to surprise Darren)… she pressed a return call button instantly so it was unlikely to be detected by Wilkinson. The risk here was that Wilkinson would hear Darren answer the phone. Emily suddenly turned assertive. She needed Darren to hear this.

She glanced at her phone and observed it answered. She shouted "WHY ARE YOU KIDNAPPING ME YOU W****R!" Wilkinson stepped forward to try and appeal to Emily that this isn't a bad situation but suddenly Emily started screaming.

"I'M NOT GOING TO HURT YOU. I JUST WANT US TO BE TOGETHER."

Darren heard all of that. He hung up and instantly phoned the police.

7 minutes later four police cars and 10 armed police descended on Emily's home. The front door wasn't even locked so they simply entered Emily's home. As armed police piled into the snooker room Wilkinson (for about 2 seconds) threatened them with a snooker cue before the reality of his pathetic situation entered his pea sized brain. The police order him to the ground and then handcuff him before taking him away.

If for Emily there is anything positive to be taken from this incident, it was that Wilkinson was useless at kidnapping. He is too nice.

"We are so sorry Miss Walsh" said one of the police.

"Oh don't worry. It was my ideal kidnapping. We just played loads of snooker."

"Still, it must have been a frightening ordeal."

"Fear of the unknown… I don't think he had any plan of what to do at all. But tha made me fear he would choose to do something violent like take a knife to my throat if Darren came round. But I don't think he was like that. I don't think he ha it in him. I mean when you guys stormed in he didn't put a knife to my throat. I think he's just a sad, lonely, pathetic loser. And that's a relief to me. Thank you fc saving me though."

"Your friend Darren Taylor called us."

"Yeah, I know."

"This will make the press you know."

"Yeah, I know that too."

A couple of hours later, with Darren now with her, Emily Walsh's house was surrounded by the British news media. By the next morning the American news media had joined the fun.

"You know what this reminds me of Darren?"

"I think so but you tell me."

"Not being able to get out of my house and go into New York City because of rioters and people trying to leave the City."

"Yup, locked in again".

"Will you do something for me Darren?"

"Of course."

"Go out there and tell the news media that I will release a statement if they promise to leave after just 3 questions from them after I have finished the statement. I assume ITV are there. I liked the GMB interview so I think its right to choose them for one of the questions. I loved the Sky Sports News interview. If they are there I will take one from them. I guess they'll just bring Sky News though so I will take my second question from them. And if the New York Times are here one from them."

Darren approached the news media outside of Emily's home. Sky Sports were not here but the other three news networks were. Emily opened the front door and a moment later she must have had 6 month's worth of photographs taken of her... all ready for the online and offline news outlets. She was now live on multiple TV News Programs from BBC, ITV, and Sky News in the UK, to CNN, Fox, and even News Nation in the U.S. cut into their non-stop Post Disclosure World news for this.

Emily's Statement to the News Media: "This was a useless attempt at taking me hostage. I wouldn't be too hard on Eddie Wilkinson. Clearly the authorities have to ensure he can't do this again but I honestly think he is just a loser, not a violent and evil man. If I am wrong about that then of course, come down on him like a ton of bricks. But he didn't lay a finger on me and he didn't seem very smart. Most people who have been kidnapped probably go through 10,000 times worse an ordeal than I did. All I had to do.... to outsmart him.... was to challenge him to snooker games. And when the armed police turned up he momentarily thought about taking them on with one of my snooker cues. Thankfully the cue is doing o and didn't have to be shot. I am now looking forward to the start of the World Championship and beating John Higgins in the First Round and beating Ronnie C Sullivan in the final assuming the Rocket reaches the final. Now I will take a question from ITV News, then Sky News, then the New York Times."

"Tom Bradby, ITV News. How did Wilkinson get in your home?"

"He must have been following me. I was out jogging, I fell, injured my knee [Emily shows her injured knee] and he was so nice and caring, pretending to be a doctor. He pretended to not know who I was. He helped me back home. I invited him in. I know its seems naive. But it seemed like it would be rude to tell him to clear off. It was like he was being a decent human being."

Bradby tried to ask another question but Emily shouted "Sky News."

"Martin Brunt, Sky News: How did you manage to inform the Police?"

"I didn't. Darren Taylor phoned me up. When I hung up I quickly pressed a phon last caller button. I then shouted things like Why are you kidnapping me and I wa screaming so that Darren would know this was serious. He will have heard it and phoned the police. New York Times."

"Jane Adams: New York Times. So Darren Taylor is a hero. How do you think th hero will do in the World Championship?"

"I think he will get his ass kicked by Selby. Naturally I kicked Selby's ass at the Athletic Club now named the Emily Walsh Snooker Club" Emily said with a smile. She allowed another question from Adams…

"And what about Wilkinson's snooker. Was he any good?"

"Wilkinson said his highest break is 42. I think that he was lying. He is a terrible player and his attempt to play snooker was the biggest crime he committed this morning."

The news media was fascinated by what would happen to the madman. Wilkinson confessed he had kidnapped Emily and intended to hold her hostage until 20th April when the World Championship starts. He was regarded as obsessed. His house was full of online and offline editions of magazine and newspaper reports on Emily Walsh and photographs of her. Those cuttings covered the walls of his entire home. He was considered mentally ill and as a result was sectioned where he would have to be rehabilitated before being freed.

The news media, which is not something that Emily rates very highly, nevertheless pleased her with their general reporting on this incident as their general message was that Emily outsmarted Wilkinson and wiped the floor with him at snooker.

Darren had unsurprisingly (given the circumstances) rushed round to Emily's. And stayed for a long time. They discussed the upcoming World Championship as Darren plays tomorrow on the opening day whereas Emily has to wait until the day after. Darren was very impressed with the young woman that Emily was maturing into given all of her past mental health issues. Her confidence to move to the UK, the way she dealt with the aftermath of what was her lowest ebb when she nearly took her own life, her confidence to do television interviews and now her attitude to the stalking kidnapper, armed police and news media all at her new home in one morning staggered him.

"Were you faking your previous illness or something?"

"My Nearly dying was the shock I needed."

"What about someone like Ronnie O' Sullivan. You have watched his documentary over and over again. What does Ronnie need to do that he doesn't do?"

"You mean concerning his health?"

"Yes."

"Ronnie sometimes says he could ditch snooker but never does. The real Ronnie needs snooker. That's the truth. But his problem is that he feels like his identity is being destroyed when he loses or when the press start saying things like oh he isn the player he used to be. His identity is all about being the most naturally gifted player ever. So I accept if I beat him it will hurt him. But that is mainly because h hasn't sorted out his mental health. We see that it is his whole identity being dissociated or perceived as being taken away from him when the camera's are on him and he clearly cannot take even playing back comments in his head that were made about him slipping. We see that its like he's literally being murdered when a player just tries to beat him in a big game even if they are totally failing."

"You don't have that problem and never have had that problem?"

"Snooker is my liberation. My dissociations (identity collapses) were subconsciou or unconscious. I only realised them when they happened. But the similarity with me and Ronnie is the word 'Identity'."

"And so you are trying not to identify? In other words to merely think that there's this collective truth that isn't emotionally identified with?"

"Yes. But I have to be especially careful because my identity seems to have revolved around truth so as to be orientated."

"So it seems to be about other people needing correcting when they are biased?"

"I guess so, yes. And that is a serious mistake I have made in the past. Because its simply replacing their identity with mine. Power corrupts and that is psychological corruption. Its the same psychology that the powerful use. And look where that gets us."

"Well I think you need another category based on whether what they are being biased about matters or not? The truth doesn't have to be an important one."

"You might be right again Darren. I think though it is right to reject another person's identity but it is not right to replace. Always delete, never replace. Be aware of the Propaganda Matrix in you. So in my case, I have to be aware of the Propaganda Matrix in me. By the way I can see why I like you. You are into snooker and you are empathic towards me, thinking so much about my issues. I might have to let you beat me at snooker one day. Shame that Selby won't let you win tomorrow though. You won't get through to the second round so I won't be able to kick your ass at the Crucible."

"I am just ecstatic to be playing at the Crucible. I will be only the second American to ever do so. Then the next day you become the first woman and the third American to ever do so."

"I got a call from Stephen Hendry. He said that the Crucible announcer is going to call me the Newbie from New York, Wonder-woman herself, EMMMIIILLLY WALSH!"

"Ha, nice. I wonder how they will announce my arrival?"

"He's here one minute, gone the next, its Darren Taylor"

"Very funny" replies Darren while turning on the TV. He wants to see if Emily is making big news. Her kidnapping is a huge story and in normal times would be dominating the news… but the news from New York City is that there is a UFO hovering over Manhattan. And more people are trying to leave again in panic.

" Lucky we left" says Darren.

Emily sighs and says "It could be a simulation so that the authorities get trusted again, get their power back that they have lost in recent years. But it could also be real. The authorities lie on issues that involve their power so we cannot know wha the truth is."

Darren wants to keep talking about the Post Disclosure World. But Emily wants t go back to the mental health issue. She says

"You have really got me thinking about identifying with truth. I had never though about the value of truth. Because you are right. It might not matter on many thing I will have to add that to my system but its never as easy as it sounds due to habitual response."

"Your mind won't be thinking about mental health tomorrow and the day after an for the next several days… the World Championship will be everything to you!"

"Yup, John Higgins, here we come. And I am hitting the Crucible's Practice table tomorrow. I can't wait I am buzzing."

8. The World Championship

Steve Davis, the best player in the world back in the 1980s, is mingling around the Crucible, seeing who is hanging around.

Emily is practising on a Crucible table.

"Hey it's the legendary Emily Walsh!" shouts Davis.

"Hey it's the legendary Steve Davis."

"Ermm, Emily, I've got some bad news. There's rumours of an alien invasion and the Government has ordered a lockdown."

"You have got to be kidding!"

"Yeah, I am. Ha ha ha"

Emily pretends to go and whack him one with her snooker cue. Steve ducks just in case she's really going to do it.

Emily takes revenge by saying "1985" and raising the cue above her head and celebrating Dennis Taylor style. She then positions the white and black exactly like it was in the famous Steve Davis missed shot and then looks up at Steve and asks

"How did you miss?"

She felt that her and Steve were now squits and so they laid off the banter and played a practise match which Emily won 104–29. Steve told her that she plays genius level snooker but said he can't hang around any longer as he is working for the BBC covering the World Championship. He also told Emily that at the first opportunity he would say on the BBC Program that he is highly confident that Walsh will be the winner of this years World Championship. Indeed, most of the snooker community were tipping her to win. A few still thought O' Sullivan. Maybe they just couldn't believe a young female American could really be as amazing as people were saying she is.

Minutes later live on the BBC Davis said that Walsh is not only the first woman to compete at the Crucible, but the first ever woman he thinks will win the thing outright. And the first ever American to win the Championship. Davis says the practice match he just played against her illustrated her talent.

"She hit a 90 break at lightening speed. It was like playing against Ronnie at his very best...She…"

John Virgo wants to speak. So he interrupts Steve in full flow by saying

"I cannot wait to see this girl play. She is by far the most interesting, indeed fascinating story in snooker history. She has won nothing yet but she has an army of fans like I have never seen before in this sport. She has done so much already to boost snooker in this country."

By the end of Day 1 the second American ever to play at the Crucible, Darren Taylor was out, losing 10–1 to Mark Selby. Enough said!

The next day on the 21st April 2024 it was Emily Walsh's turn. Crowds had gathered outside of the Crucible Arena, with fans chanting EMILY EMILY EMILY. But the capacity of the Crucible is just under 1,000 so the vast majority of them could not get in. The one's who did get in loved announcers Rob Walkers welcome:

"She's the Newbie from New York, Wonder-woman herself, EMMMIIILLLY WALSH!"

When Walker welcomed John Higgins into the arena the crowd were still chanting "EMILY EMILY EMILY", and waving American flags.

The crowd erupted and started chanting. Seconds later the referee was raising his own voice shouting

"Quiet Please. Please, be quiet for the players."

"First frame, Emily Walsh to break."

17 million British people had tuned in on TV for this match. The highest UK snooker television viewing figure for a snooker match since the Davis v Taylor final in 1985. But Walsh v Higgins was only a first round match!

Her first ever shot in the Crucible was a standard break off. But when Higgins played his first shot as a safety she came back to the table and made a fantastic pot anyway. The crowd erupted with cheers. And from there she went on to make a break of 107 winning the first frame. Co-commentator Stephen Hendry said *"The century breaks, cue-ball control, safety game, temperament, the killer instinct, she's got it all…"*

Incredibly Walsh made 4 century+ breaks blowing Higgins away 10–3. And on her final frame she made a 147 break in just 6 minutes 58 seconds. Frequently throughout the match the referee had to call on the crowd to quieten down. It really was almost like a Wimbledon tennis atmosphere. On leaving the Crucible around 3,000 fans mobbed Walsh. The question now was who would she face in the next round? The answer was Stuart Bingham. And Emily won 13–0 in what was described by the snooker family as the greatest performance by the most majestic talent ever seen in a match of snooker. Walsh made six century breaks and again made a 147, although she took over 8 minutes to make the maximum break.

When she went home that night she was with Darren yet again. The news media were spreading untrue rumours about them being together as a couple. Taylor is married. Heaven knows what his wife thinks about the endless rumors about his relationship with Emily Walsh. Although the news was even more interested in rumours being put out there by various UFO researchers (who remember now had more respect than they used to) about all kinds of weird Mi-Lab style unethical abductions of humans and otherworldly simulated events. They were providing at least some evidence though in terms of a clear and obvious increase in the number of people (across all demographics) reporting these strange otherworldly experiences happening to themselves.

"Turn the news off" said Emily "and let's just relax with some wine."

"Sounds like a good idea" responded Darren.

Emily's quarter final match is a few days away. But the day after Emily's 13–0 win over Bingham, Ronnie O' Sullivan was interviewed by Hazel Irvine. It's the first time that O' Sullivan is asked about Walsh. He said

"She hardly ever misses. She has no snooker nerves. The only fault I can see is that even she occasionally has bad luck, for example after playing a great shot but the white flicks off a ball that was in the way of perfect positioning and ends up rolling into the pocket for a foul. In about 40 or 50% of her games she plays almost as good as I did in my 5 minutes 8 seconds 147. So the key, if I get to play against her, is to get the first pot in, and to get among the balls so that I can build up a high break. If she's not at the table there's nothing she can do. But therefore I have to be scoring high and playing the best snooker of my life."

"If you get to play against her the viewing figures will be huge. She won the BBC 17 million viewers in her first round match and 19 million in the second round."

Emily's Quarter Final was against Luca Brecel. She won 13–5. Brecel tried to play like Ronnie O' Sullivan said he would try and play against Walsh but it was to no avail. The viewing figures were a record 21 million for that match. And the crowds outside the Crucible were estimated at 10,000. Then in the Semi Final Walsh won 17–7 against Mark Williams, with 23 million BBC viewers and an estimated 12,000 fans outside the Crucible. Meanwhile O' Sullivan also won his semi final 17–7 against Mark Selby and the world got the final they had craved all along. Emily Walsh vs Ronnie O' Sullivan.

The final was scheduled for 5th May 2024, rolling over to 6th May 2024. An estimated 22,000 fans were outside the Crucible and when the two snooker genius' arrived they were greeted like rock stars. The estimated TV viewing figures were set to reach 30 million, more like an England national football teams viewing figures in a World Cup Semi Final or Final than a snooker match. The crowd inside were also becoming more like a football match. Previous matches had experienced tennis style atmospheres that had to be quietened down to snooker level atmospheres. It would be remarkably difficult, maybe impossible to quieten this crowd to what is expected of a snooker crowd. The Rocket still had his fans but the chants of EMILY EMILY EMILY were at full volume 1 hour before the start of the match.

"This is bonkers" remarked John Virgo in the BBC Studio.

Then came the moment the world had been waiting for… the introduction of the players and the start of the biggest snooker match in history.

"She's the Newbie from New York, Wonder-woman herself, EMMMIIILLLY WALSH!"

!!!EMILY EMILY EMILY!!! chanted the crowd.

"And he's the 7 times World Champion, and he's the Rocket, RONNNIE O SULLLIVANNNN!"

Cheers went up but the EMILY chanting had continued.

There was then a 5 minute delay as the Referee pleaded with the crowd to quieten down. The ref failed to quieten the crowd and Emily broke off to a crescendo of EMILY EMILY EMILY chanting.

Over the next 20 or so minutes Walsh experienced something she had never experienced before. She went 2–0 down in frames to O' Sullivan as the Rockets hope of getting among the balls first had come to pass. And he made fast 77 and 8 breaks thus was playing his best snooker. But Emily won the next two frames to make it 2–2 with breaks of 101 and 69 only for Ronnie to go 3–2 up. Then Walsh hit form winning 4 games on the bounce in just 40 minutes. O Sullivan pulled a frame back and the first day finished at 6–4 to Walsh.

On Day 2, Walsh started amazingly making a 147 in the very first frame to go 7–4 up. It seemed like Walsh might run away with it at that point but O' Sullivan pulled a frame back straight away. (7–5). Over the next 10 frames Walsh won 5 and O' Sullivan won 5 making it 12–10. But then Walsh hit her best form of the match so far scoring 3 century breaks in a row to go 15–10 in-front. The next frame was won by O Sullivan (15–11) but then in the next frame O' Sullivan made a break of 70 and then missed with 71 points still on the table. Walsh cleared up to make it 16–11. She was now just two frames away from becoming 2024 World Champion. The crowd were louder than ever… chanting and cheering and even stamping feet. Walsh won the next frame to go 17–11 up and then like a miracle in the final frame she made yet another 147 break in just 5 minutes and 2 seconds, beating Ronnie O' Sullivan's 5 minutes 8 seconds record and winning her the World Championship.

The New Y[...]

7th May 2024

Walsh is World Champion

19 year old Emily Walsh is World Snooker Champion following beating the Rocket Ronnie O Sullivan 18-11 at the Crucible. Walsh actually lost the first two frames as the Rocket hit excellent early form. But day 1 finished 6-4 to Walsh. 30 million people had tuned into the BBC to watch this match, considered by the world to be the biggest snooker match in history. On Day 2, Walsh started amazingly making a 147 in the very first frame to go 7-4 up. It seemed like Walsh might run away with it at that point but O Sullivan pulled a frame back straight away (7-5). Over the next 10 frames Walsh won 5 and O Sullivan won 5 making it 12-10. But then Walsh hit her best form of the match so far scoring 3 century breaks in a row to go 15-10 in-front. The next frame was won by O Sullivan (15-11) but then in the next frame O Sullivan made a break of 70 and then missed with 71 points still on the table, Walsh cleared up to make it 16-11. She was now just 2 frames away from becoming 2024 World Champion. The crowd were louder

[text cut off: Re... foll... imp... The... that rela... the... beh... of a... exp... in l... its... beh... con... or v... It m... tota... thir... dec... mos...]

The celebrations from her fans outside the Crucible were extraordinary for snooker. Again, it can only be compared to football style hero worship. In UK terms she was A-list. She was also well known in New York City but they were to consumed with UAP Disclosure for her to become quite as big there as she is in th UK.

Emily was walking back to her Sheffield home when suddenly the world all aroun her transformed.

"Wait, what?!?" she said out-loud.

Suddenly she was back in New York City and there was no anarchy, no rioting, not even any protesting. But this is impossible thought Emily. One second ago I was in Sheffield, England. Absolutely stunned she headed for her old Brooklyn home and wondered what the hell she was going to find there. She walked in the front door which was open. And there was Jennifer Rush, the reporter she had hit on resulting in Emily's overdose and near death. Jennifer came over to her, kissed Emily on the lips and said

"Welcome back home Emily." She pours Emily a glass of wine but Emily, stunned, totally ignores it.

"Are we together?" asked Emily, completely not understanding her own question because she was well aware that they were not.

Jennifer replied "Of course. We are in love… aren't we?"

"I am living in the UK now" Emily shouts with a gobsmacked impression on her face.

Puzzled Jennifer responds "Last time I checked New York was still part of the U.S."

"It's funny, just the other night I was challenging myself to not identify with truth because if truth is always getting challenged and regarded as not the truth even though I think it is then if its your whole identity you will mentally collapse every-time truth is called not the truth."

"I think I would need to hear that again to understand. But your point is?"

"Well this is the best example of what I consider to be NOT the truth…. I mean… [Emily bursts out laughing and blinking as if when her eyes re-open she'll be back in Sheffield]."

"Are you ok Emily? You said you have got over the worst of your symptoms. Have you been drinking again?"

Emily looked at Jennifer and then asked

"Would you mind if I just have some time alone to gather my thoughts?"

"Of course, but give me a shout if something is bothering you."

Emily goes upstairs thinking something is more than bothering me!!!! She sits on her old bed and ponders what the hell is going on??? Her reference point is the UFO issue. She thinks about what her theories are... basically we are being played by the Propaganda Matrix. The UFO/NHI stuff could be real or could be a Psy-Op She said the UFO over NYC could be a simulation of a UFO. She was vaguely aware of simulated MI-Lab style abductions. Something involving the Post Disclosure World... the intelligence that has brought all of this about is playing with her, and surely also manipulating other people too. Well maybe its worth identifying with truth at this level she thought. But even now, so profound an impact has subconscious identifying had on her life for the worse, that she makes special exception concerning basic orientation of reality not transforming into Alice (or in this case) Emily in Wonderland. The crucible crowd would say Wonder-woman in Wonderland. But this was not the Crucible. This was not Sheffield. This was not England. This was New York. Or its simulated New York Emily wasn't sure at all.

She goes back downstairs to face Jennifer again.

"Jennifer, I nearly killed myself over the incident with you. Nearly dying was a massive shock to my system. I am now living in England and I am World Snooke Champion."

Jennifer didn't respond. Then the world transformed again and she was in an infinite dark void where there was only Emily's consciousness. Fear engulfed her as she looked around for something, anything.

"Am I going to be stranded here forever???"

She wanted to scream but screaming in the Void would be futile. But maybe she could spend as long as it takes to work through her issues here? Well she would have to get over the worst fear of her life first. You cannot think when you are as terrified as Emily is right now. But then there was something to grasp at. She heard a voice, a man's voice repetitively calling her name. It was Darren.

"Emily, wake up." Emily's eyes popped open. She wondered what the hell she had just experienced. Maybe her subconscious had wanted to work out the truth about the UFO issue.

"I had such a weird and realistic nightmare, that was more real than real" said Emily speaking excitedly. There was a sudden transformation of reality and I was back in New York City and Jennifer Rush and I were lovers."

"Well you really are World Champion and the greatest snooker player who ever lived. It might seem like a weird dream but its totally real."

Emily had slept in by a couple of hours and Darren was aware that Stephen Hendry was calling round.

Hendry called round in an eccentric chitty chitty bang bang-esque car. They went for a drive outside the city and into the countryside blasting out ABBA's *Money Money Money* to get her into the mood of her new lifestyle.

9. Emily Walsh and the Phenomenon

Eddie Wilkinson was not an obsessive Emily Walsh fan. The CIA had paid him
$1.5 million to inject Emily with an implant that would enable the CIA to always
know exactly where she was. They would then be able to make her experience
highly disorientating otherworldly super real simulated events. His arrest was
exactly what was supposed to happen. Wilkinson is a British serial killer who
carried out his killings while on holiday in the U.S. before he flew back to the UK.
The CIA had been collecting criminals who had carried out how risk crimes to do
their dirty UAP/Alien related work for them… in return for huge amounts of
money and either being let off for their crimes, or in this case, receiving very light
consequences relative to what would have been the death sentence for mass murde
in the States. The CIA had plastered the walls of Wilkinson's home with Emily
Walsh magazine and newspaper cuttings in order to fool the UK authorities. They
could of got him off scott-free, with no loss of freedom whatsoever but the CIA at
least wanted some consequences for what he had done in the U.S. Emily herself
was totally fooled as well. She thought he was a non-violent obsessed fan who
went too far. In truth he was responsible for the murder of 12 Americans. He had
been trained by the CIA and thus when he helped Emily to her feet after she fell he
injected the implant and Emily mistook the millisecond sharp pain for pain that ha
been caused by her fall.

Emily Walsh was one of thousands of people selected by the CIA for implant
tracking and for being messed with in terms of simulated otherworldly
experiences. Walsh, like all of the others subjected to this, was chosen because sh
had a public profile and the CIA thought that in the context of the UFO issue bein

accepted in the Post Disclosure world that they would almost all eventually speak out, thus cementing the view of the worlds population that the UFO/Alien presence is totally real.

The CIA's plan worked. It was all done, just as Emily theorized might be the case, so as to regain the establishment's loss of authority. They had feared a revolution and wanted the public to trust power again. Thus they got the ball rolling on bringing about more respect for the UFO issue, even fooling Blink 182 rock star, Tom Delonge into thinking this was all real. One or two from inside the CIA acted like early whistle-blowers, most notably Lue Elizondo. Later David Grusch who used to brief the President on national security matters would play a similar role. The Disclosure Act was passed, the President rubber stamped it, thus official Disclosure was enacted. Then, to cement it the CIA messed with thousands of public figures such as celebrities.

But Emily Walsh never did speak out. This was because she couldn't determine whether her world-transforming experiences were real or something like the CIA messing with her head. Her suspicion of power had served her well. But her life was cut short when, aged 32 she was tragically gunned down by Eddie Wilkinson. The Crucible in Sheffield which had already seen its capacity increased due to the popularity that Walsh had single-handedly brought to the sport... was re-named in her honor as... THE EMILY WALSH ARENA.

She was the greatest snooker player who ever lived.

NOTES/CREDITS

1. Netflix drama *The Queen's Gambit* is credited with the quote "To tell you the truth Emily, you're astounding." 1 minute 41 seconds into this video you see/hear Mr Shaibel say to Beth Harmon "To tell you the truth of it child, you're astounding." <u>Beth & Mr. Shaibel | "Am I good enough now?" —</u> <u>YouTube</u>

2. In Chapter 5 Emily discussed Collective Truth using pop culture as her example. More specifically she turned her attention to the coolest music artists and said that the question of what is cool concerning music artists is something that is collectively determined so that conversation and relating t others be possible. Emily was referring to a real life British study, see here: <u>Rock band Queen voted 'coolest' artists — while Cliff Richard tops 'uncoo</u> <u>list — Mirror Online</u>

3. In Chapter 8 I write Emily takes revenge by saying "1985" and raising the cue above her head and celebrating Dennis Taylor style. She then positions the white and black exactly like it was in the famous Steve Davis missed shot and then looks up at Steve and asks "How did you miss?" The *how did you miss* question is about the miss (at 2 minutes 59 seconds point) of this video. <u>09 Taylor And Davis's Black Ball Finish — YouTube</u>

4. In Chapter 8 Stephen Hendry says *"The century breaks, cue-ball control, safety game, temperament, the killer instinct, she's got it all…"* He really di say that in real life… except Hendry said *"he's"* got it all" because it was with reference to Ronnie O' Sullivan. See here: <u>SG Reviews: Unbreakable</u> <u>by Ronnie O'Sullivan and Tom Fordyce — Sports Gazette</u>

5. All snooker players mentioned in this book, with the exception of the main character, are snooker players in real life. That includes the American players. See United States National Snooker Championship — Wikipedia

By the same author

Abduction Inspired UFO Disclosure is only the Start

★★★★☆

Synopsis

Sarah Aston is falling out of love with her husband, Mike, and at the same time she is having strange nightmares or maybe, actual UFO abductions. Her best friend, the scheming Lara Hine, who wants Sarah for herself as her girlfriend, gets her wish and both she and Sarah then experience shared UFO related contact phenomena. Indeed, it would seem much of the worlds population are becoming experiencers. This leads to Disclosure of some exotic Other intelligence although it remains unclear what the exact origins of the exotic Others are. (For example, ETs? Simulators? Time Travelers? Interdimensionals?) Lara certainly knows much more than she admits. Eventually she starts to talk. But is she telling the truth?

Reviewed by Stewart Bint (Author of Timeshaft)

I originally read this four-chapter book out of order. By that, I mean, chapters three and four before one and two. Why, I hear you ask?

Author Paul Budding had asked if I would take a look at his two short stories, published on an open writers website. They were to become chapters three and four of his 29,000-word book, Abduction Inspired UFO Disclosure is Only the Start.

I was totally intrigued by the concept of his stories, so I went on to read the whole book which was supplied to me free of charge by the author, in exchange for an honest review.

The overall sci-fi and conspiracy theory story arc is epic, and as far as I know, unique. I'm giving it four stars, having deducted one on two counts.

First: prolific author Jeffrey Archer always says: "Don't call me a writer, because I'm not. I'm a storyteller." And Paul Budding is definitely a fine storyteller with a fine story to tell. But I'd have preferred to see much more 'show' instead of tell. More 'show' would have added better writing to that storyteller tag.

Second: While the concept of this book is a completely new sweeping idea, I personally think the author is missing a huge trick by restricting this mammoth saga to such a short novel.

I believe the author has the idea and potential material for a multi-book series of full-length novels. And by full-length, I mean three books of between 80,000 and 100,000 words each.

Chapters one and two could combine and be expanded to become the first full-length novel introducing the two central characters, showing how they meet and fall in love. This would allow intricate world-building, showing, rather than telling readers, how the UFO Post-Disclosure World came about.

With expansion and development, the third chapter, Lara The Flawed Genius, could become a second full-length novel, with the fourth chapter developing into the final book of the trilogy.

The world-building we have in Abduction Inspired UFO Disclosure is Only the Start is superb, but there is so much untapped story lying beneath the surface.

In my opinion, and remember that's all it is - just my personal opinion - Paul Budding's storytelling is superb, but an editor's eye could tighten up the writing. For example, there's the occasional change of tense from past to present - once even in the same paragraph.

I'd just like to see that full story arc reach its true potential in a trilogy of professionally edited full-length novels.

Having said all this, though, the book as it stands now, fully merits the four stars I've given it, and I thoroughly recommend it to fans of sci-fi and conspiracy theories. Definitely one to get your teeth into.

Printed in Great Britain
by Amazon